MARC BROWN
ARTHUR'S
FIRST SLEEPOVER

LITTLE, BROWN AND COMPANY
New York ⤳ Boston

For the cousins, Katharine, Jonathan,
Hayley, Shea, and Miles, with love

Little, Brown and Company

Hachette Book Group USA
237 Park Avenue, New York, NY 10017
Visit our Web site at www.lb-kids.com

First Paperback Edition

Library of Congress Cataloging-in-Publication Data

Brown, Marc Tolon.
    Arthur first sleepover / Marc Brown. — 1st ed.
       p.   cm.
    Summary: Rumors about sightings of an alien spaceship create
excitement when Arthur's friends come to spend the night.
    ISBN 0-316-11049-3
    [1. Sleepovers — Fiction. 2. Aardvark — Fiction]   I. Title.
PZ7.B81618Apn   1994
[E] — dc20   93-46113

20 19 18 17 16 15 14 13

SC
Manufactured in China

Arthur was getting ready for his first sleepover.
"It isn't until Saturday," called Mother. "Come in and eat your breakfast."

Father laughed while he read the paper.
"Some man in town says he saw a spaceship," he chuckled.
"Probably the same man who thinks he saw Elvis at the mall,"
joked Mother.
"I don't believe in aliens," said Arthur.
"Well, the *National Requirer* does," said D.W., "and they'll pay a
lot of money for a picture of one!"

On the way to school the girls were talking about the
spaceship.
Arthur wanted to talk about his sleepover.
"We can have the sleepover in my tent!" said Arthur.
"You wouldn't catch me out in a tent with these spaceships
landing," said Muffy.

"Bad news," said Buster. "My mom thinks I'm too young for a sleepover. I can't come."

"But you have to," said Arthur. "It's my first sleepover and you're my best friend."

"Why do they call them sleepovers?" said Francine. "No one ever sleeps."

That afternoon Arthur told his mother about Buster's problem.
"Well, I'll see what I can do," said Mother.
Arthur crossed his fingers while she dialed.
Buster's mom did all the talking.
"Yes. No. Of course not," said Mother. "Absolutely. Good talking with you, too. 'Bye."
Mother smiled and nodded her head yes.

"Hooray!" cried Arthur.
"Does Buster's mom know about the spaceship?" asked D.W.
"I saw flashing lights from one today."
"I think that was the Pizza Shop sign," said Mother.

Saturday morning Arthur was outside making the tent cozy for his sleepover. His family helped too.
"I was just thinking," said D.W. "How do we know you're our real parents and not aliens in their bodies?"

"Did you brush your teeth?" asked Father.
"And pick up that mess in your room, young lady," said
Mother.
"Okay, okay," said D.W.
"They sound real to me," said Arthur.

Arthur was looking for his flashlight when Buster and the Brain arrived. "It was here a minute ago," said Arthur.
"I wonder if you'll see any aliens," said D.W.
"If we do," said the Brain, "how will we communicate with them?"

"Forget about communicating," said D.W. "Take pictures for the *National Requirer!* Use my camera. We can split the money."

"Let's make some signs," said Arthur.

"Good idea," said Buster. "But first I have to call my mom."

After they finished their signs, they unpacked.
"I brought a few snacks," said the Brain.
"I brought a rubber snake," said Arthur, "to keep D.W. away.
What did you bring, Buster?"
"Just my baseball cards," said Buster, "and my blankie."
"Do you think we really *will* see aliens tonight?"
"No. Do you?" said Arthur.
"Highly unlikely," said the Brain.

The boys forgot all about aliens.
They were too busy telling jokes and trading baseball cards.
"Pillow fight!" screamed Buster.
"Quiet," said the Brain. "What's that sound?"
"Footsteps," whispered Buster.

"And they're getting closer," said Arthur. "Oh! Oh!"
"Pizza delivery," called an unfamiliar voice.
"Compliments of the sleepover parents."
Everyone laughed.
"I almost stopped breathing," said Arthur.
"I almost wet my pants!" said Buster.

Before they knew it, they heard another voice.
"Lights out!" said Father. "It's after nine. Bedtime."
"Already?" said Arthur.
"Thank you for the pizza, sir," said the Brain.
"You're welcome," said Father. "Good night."
"Good night," said the boys sweetly.

As soon as they heard Father go back into the house, they shot out of their sleeping bags like cannonballs.
"I heard bedtime," said the Brain, "but I didn't hear sleeptime!"
"Let's tell spooky stories," said Arthur.
"How about cards?" suggested Buster.

Just as it was Arthur's turn to go fish, they saw the flashing lights.
They dropped their cards.
It got very quiet.
"Aliens!" whispered Buster.
"I don't hear any footsteps," whispered Arthur.
"Of course not," said the Brain. "They haven't landed yet."
Lights flashed again.
"They're headed for our tent! Run for your life!"

No one could find the flaps.
"Help!" screamed Buster. "Let me out!"
The tent collapsed.
That didn't stop them from making a run for it.
But a large maple tree did.
"Ouch!" said Arthur.
"I'm calling my mom," said Buster.

"Look!" said the Brain. "The lights are coming from your house!"
"I think I know this alien," said Arthur. "It's from the planet D.W.!"
Arthur noticed the things they used to make signs.
That gave him an idea.
"Let's put our tent back up. I think I know a way we can teach
that little space creature a lesson."

Later, Arthur crept quietly into the house.
D.W. was in her room laughing.
"What's so funny?" he asked.
"What are you doing up here?" said D.W.
"Did you come in because you're scared?"

"Not really," said Arthur. "I'm returning your camera.
You'll probably see an alien before we will."
"I doubt it," said D.W.
"Well, just in case," said Arthur. "Sweet dreams."
Then, very quietly, he returned to his tent.

A minute later D.W. heard a tap at her window.
"Aliens!" she screamed.
She screamed so loud it woke up everyone in the
neighborhood.
Everyone except Buster, the Brain, and Arthur.
When Mother and Father went out to check, the boys
were sleeping like little angels.

Of course, after Mother and Father went back into the house, it was another story.